By R.P. Huttinga

The Adventures Of
Aussie and Otis

Winter Storm

Otis sat by the patio door, watching Mrs. B rake the leaves. He watched as the last golden maple leaves slowly danced to the ground.

Otis turned to Aussie. "Why do the leaves fall off the trees?" he asked her.

Aussie told him, "The trees are getting ready for winter."

Mrs. B leaned her rake against the tree. She walked over to the patio door to let the dogs out. Aussie slowly got up, but not Otis—he came charging out the door with great speed. He jumped off the deck, leaping into the air, and landed in the big pile of leaves.

"Aussie! Come and find me!" Otis yelled. Aussie slowly walked off the deck and stood in front of the pile of leaves. "Otis, I can't find you," she said.

Otis giggled.

Then Aussie saw his eyes.

"OH, THERE YOU ARE,"

she said.

Mrs. B came around the corner of the garage. She saw Otis in the pile of scattered leaves. "Oh, you little rascal," she said to Otis. "Time for you to come inside."

Otis walked slowly back to the house. He wished he could play longer. He watched as Mrs. B raked the leaves into a big pile again.

Mrs. B walked back to the house and forgot about Aussie sitting under the big maple tree. Aussie walked over to the fresh pile of leaves. It had such a wonderful smell of autumn. She looked around and started to roll in the pile of leaves. It feels so good! she thought.

Otis was sitting on his bed in the kitchen. He looked out the patio door and saw Aussie rolling in the leaves. He started barking.

Mrs. B came downstairs. "What's all the fuss about?" she asked Otis. "Do you want to go out again?"

Otis walked over to the patio door wagging his tail. Mrs. B opened the door.

Otis ran to the pile of leaves Aussie had just finished rolling in.

"That felt good," Aussie said. "It made me feel like a puppy again." She walked by Otis and headed towards the house.

When Mrs. B saw Aussie standing by the sliding door she opened it. Then she saw Otis standing by the scattered pile of leaves.

"NOT AGAIN, YOU LITTLE RASCAL!"

she yelled at Otis.

Aussie grinned as she walked past Mrs. B. Otis rolled his eyes and followed Aussie inside.

The next morning, Otis woke up early. He looked outside, and all the rooftops were covered in white. "Aussie, are you awake?" he asked softly. He was trying not to wake up Mrs. B.

"Otis. It's too early to get up," said Aussie.

"But there are big grey clouds. The sun did not come up. What's happening?" he asked her.

Aussie slowly opened her eyes and took a quick look outside. "I think we might get snow today," she said.

Otis couldn't believe it—it was going to snow! He had waited so long for this. "Aussie, you have to get up!" he said.

But Aussie was sound asleep again. Otis kept looking out the patio door, waiting to see if it would snow. But he had never seen snow before. What would it look like? he thought.

Then it started—one flake, then another, and another. Finally Otis couldn't keep count as all the flakes gently touched the ground. His little tail was wagging so fast it woke up Aussie.

Mrs. B came downstairs. "Well, what do we have here?" she said to the dogs. "I guess you will need your winter coat, Aussie."

As Mrs. B put her coat on her, Aussie loved the feel of the fleece. Otis couldn't wait any longer—he needed to touch the snow. Mrs. B opened the patio door.

Otis slowly walked onto the deck. The snow touched his belly. He stopped and looked up. A snowflake fell on his nose! It stayed there for a few seconds. Then it melted and ran down his chin.

Aussie came outside with her winter jacket on. She rolled in the snow. "The coat feels so good," she said to Otis.

Otis noticed his favorite ball by the apple trees. It was covered in snow. He started to run down the hill to get his ball. The hill was slippery. At first he was a little scared, but then he realized how much fun it was to slide in the snow. He slid down the hill over and over.

All the next night the snow fell.

Otis was the first to wake up the next morning. He walked to the patio door, but all he could see was white. Otis gently nudged Aussie. "Could you look outside?" he asked. "I don't know what happened."

Aussie yawned and walked to the patio door. "Well Otis," she said. "This is our first snow storm."

Mrs. B came downstairs and looked out the kitchen window. "Oh no," she said. "I was meaning to get more milk. I guess after we have breakfast I will go to the store."

Mrs. B waited for the storm to slow down. Then she went to the closet to get her coat and boots. She opened the door and was about to put on her gloves and toque. Otis sneaked between her legs and went outside. "Come back inside!" she told Otis.

But Otis didn't listen. This was his chance to show Mrs. B what Aussie had taught him. He walked by the garage and bumped the sleigh. It fell down and Otis grabbed the rope. He started to pull the sleigh.

Mrs. B laughed. "You're too small to be a sled dog, Otis."

Otis did not give up. He pulled the sleigh to the maple tree.

"Well, little guy," said Mrs. B, "if you think you can pull the sleigh you should try."

Mrs. B tied the rope to Otis's harness. "Ok my little sled dog, off to Mr. Wilson's store."

Mrs. B walked in front of Otis to make a trail, and Otis followed her. He looked up. The trees are wearing white sweaters, he thought. But he had to focus on being a sled dog. He remembered what Aussie had told him. "Keep your head up," he kept telling himself.

Mrs. B and Otis reached the top of the hill. That's when they saw Aspen playing in the snow in his front yard. Aspen saw Mrs. B but not Aussie. Who could be pulling the sled? he thought. Then he looked over and saw Otis shaking the snow off his little body. "Otis, is that really you pulling the sleigh?" he asked.

"Yes Aspen.

I AM A SLED DOG TODAY!"

Aspen grinned as Otis and
Mrs. B walked past his home.

When they reached the store, Otis noticed two big
piles of snow on each side of Mr. Wilson's front
doors. He remembered Mr. Wilson kept cookies under
his counter.

Mr. Wilson looked outside. He saw Otis sitting by
the sled, and he quickly put on his coat.

1605

Outside the door, he bent down and gave Otis two small cookies. "You must be tired, little fellow, pulling that sleigh all the way to my store," he said. Mr. Wilson looked inside and saw Mrs. B standing by the check-out counter. He said good bye to Otis and went back inside.

Mrs. B came back outside with two bags and gently placed them on the sleigh. She put her hands into her coat pockets to get her gloves and hat. Otis grabbed the rope with his teeth and started to pull the sleigh again. "Otis, that's too heavy for you to pull now," said Mrs. B. But Otis didn't stop, so Mrs. B tied the rope to his harness again.

When they reached Aspen's house Otis's little legs were getting tired. It's not much farther, he thought, I have to do this. Finally he could see their house. Smoke was rising from the chimney. He saw Aussie sitting by the big window in the living room. When Aussie saw Otis pulling the sleigh she got a big smile on her face.

When they came to the back door, Mrs. B untied Otis from his harness, and she opened the door to let Otis in. Otis walked over to his bed and put his little head on his pillow. He took a deep breath. Being a sled dog is a lot of work, he thought.

He was about to fall asleep when he felt Aussie pulling a fluffy blanket over his tired body. Aussie knelt down and whispered into Otis's ear, "I am so proud of you my little sled pug. Wait until we have our next adventure."

OTIS GRINNED AND FELL ASLEEP.

To learn more about Rescue Dog Organizations, please visit www.aussieandotis.com

◆ FriesenPress

Suite 300 - 990 Fort St
Victoria, BC, V8V 3K2
Canada

www.friesenpress.com

Copyright © 2018 by R.P. Huttinga
First Edition — 2018

www.aussieandotis.com

All rights reserved.

No part of this publication may be reproduced in any
form, or by any means, electronic or mechanical, including
photocopying, recording, or any information browsing,
storage, or retrieval system, without permission in writing from
FriesenPress.

ISBN
978-1-5255-1997-0 (Hardcover)
978-1-5255-1998-7 (Paperback)
978-1-5255-1999-4 (eBook)

1. JUVENILE FICTION, ANIMALS, DOGS

Distributed to the trade by The Ingram Book Company

In loving memory of Aussie
2000 - 2017

"LOOK FOR AUSSIE AND OTIS IN

"SUMMER
VACATION"

Printed in Canada